Cover image licensed by depositphotos.com/ ©Moguchev
Cover design by L.J. Anderson

Editors
Chanse Lowell
D Beck

Publication Date: June 13, 2013
Genre: FICTION/Romance
Print ISBN-13: 978-0615883724
ISBN-10: 0615883729
Copyright © 2013 K.I. Lynn
All rights reserved

DISSOLUTION

by
K.I. Lynn

Sandra,

Enjoy the BEAST!

♡ KI Lynn

The Beginning of Our End...

My chest clenched, and I rubbed the spot with firm pressure. A familiar pain was flooding in, and once again it was all my fault.

The doors to the elevator closed in front of me, the number twelve disappearing before my eyes, leaving me to stare at my own lifeless reflection. The weight of my decision hovered above me, poised for the right moment to crash down.

I saw her long before I ever met her; Lila, my cohort in crime at work and at home. Across a sea of asphalt and cars, was where I caught my first glimpse of the woman who would do the impossible and awaken a long dead part of me.

She was unassuming, skittish even, captivating me with the way she walked. There was nothing particularly special about it; maybe it was just the way the light reflected in her natural blonde hair. Whatever it was, my eyes were glued to her. She became more intriguing when her demeanor changed, as two men approached; her body rigid, pace slowed, and eyes down. It was subtle, not many would notice, but I did.

The caged beast inside me also noticed and pulled at his chains, growling. He didn't like that they made her feel that way. I was about to go to her, launch myself at her, the beast wanting the strange siren, when a hand clamped down on my shoulder and pulled me back to reality.

I shouldn't have taken the job when Jack offered it to me. In fact, the only reason I did was to have something to keep me busy, keep my mind off everything. To keep the days passing as I waited to die.

Every day was the same; a spiral down to hell. I knew my family was waiting for the call that I'd offed myself. I'd been tempted, hundreds of times, but I never went through with it.

I wished I had. Better to destroy myself, and not take her with me.

The throbbing behind my ribs was damn near crippling and made my legs shaky, as I tried to brace myself in the elevator while it moved. No one would ever find out the level of asshole I'd achieved.

I'd done it. Done what I thought I couldn't.

I left her…the one good thing I had in my purgatory.

So, why did it hurt so bad that my eyes stung? I could barely breathe or think. Shouldn't I have been proud I finally found the inner strength to do what was best for her?

I blinked and swallowed, but the lump of shame in my throat wouldn't budge.

2

It was a necessary separation. I couldn't keep hurting her, and that night I *physically* hurt her.

She deserved more, so much more than me; an angry, depressed, broken man. I couldn't give her what she needed—love. So, I did what I had asked her to do.

I left.

Once more my eyes stung like a son of a bitch, but there was no room for tears. I didn't deserve them.

Visions of her collapsed and passed out after I lost control and took her, assaulted me. It'd been too much, too rough. I begged her to leave, told her I couldn't control it. Not today.

Today was the day it all resurfaced. The pain, the agony…*my wife.*

The life, the love, and the family that was taken from me.

The last time I saw her surfaced. Her eyes open; staring, blank, void, empty…dead.

The medically induced coma they placed me in kept me from even saying goodbye. I was unable to attend her funeral.

The elevator signaled that I reached my floor, and I was left with heavy steps as I walked out and down the hall. I entered my condo after having deposited Lila back into hers, leaving her.

I shut the door behind me, leaning on it as it clicked closed. All of my belongings I'd retrieved from her place dropped to the ground, landing on the tile floor below.

My hands moved to my hair, tugging and pulling on it as the air around me became suffocating. I felt something

3

digging into my palm and released my grip to find out what it was.

I opened my hand and in it rested a jagged piece of metal.

Her key...the key to my place. I took it from her key ring and returned the one she'd given me.

The weight was becoming too much, almost crippling. The animal inside me was stirring, the part of me that wanted her more than I wanted to admit.

Gone. She was gone. I left.

Mine! The beast howled. *She. Is. Mine!*

"No. She deserves to be happy and loved. I can't give her that."

I leaned my forehead on the door, pounding my fist on it—hoping the door would give way and I'd have an excuse to run back to her. Any excuse to end the agony in which I was beginning to drown.

"Stay here! You have to."

Arguing with myself probably couldn't be seen as sane, but my head and heart were warring. My feelings for her had become so strong.

Mine! He roared.

"Lila..."

Mine!

"Oh, God, what have I done?" I doubled over, the crushing weight of my actions coming down on me. "I need you. I need you so much."

Get. Her. Back!

"I can't. No. I won't...I won't hold her down, hold her back. Someone will worship the ground she walks on, love her."

We *can do that. No one will ever understand her like we do.*

"Someone will try. Someone will want and love her."

Someone like Andrew?

My voice broke down to a whisper. "Yes, someone like Andrew."

No! Mine. Not Andrew's. Mine. I need her!

A crunching sound that had become all too familiar in recent months filled my ears. I looked down to find my hand embedded in the drywall.

My knuckles began to sting as I stared at my arm still lodged in the new hole. I pulled my hand out and surveyed the damage. I spun around, looking at all of the holes that the entry walls contained. All were created because of her. Because I wanted her and tried to deny it. Because I wouldn't face the truth about what was going on between us. Because I was angry at her for making me feel for her.

That was the moment I came crumbling apart at the seams.

I grabbed at the edge of the drywall and pulled, tearing a chunk from the wall.

It wasn't enough. In a frantic pace I began pulling, large pieces coming off in my hands. The dust filled the air, clouding it, just like my mind and my heart. I needed the reminder of her gone.

I'd gotten one section down before it let loose; the pain, the loss, the anger. Nothing was safe from my path of destruction.

I pulled half a sheet down in one tug, tossed it to the side and manically finished the demolition of the remaining, offending plasterboard.

5

Every tug, every pull, I tried to push her memory away. The feel of her skin, her body beneath mine, her smile, her laughter, her mind, her taste, her need.

She needed me. I knew that. I needed her; something I was just beginning to understand.

I left. Separating us.

I screamed out, cursing myself, my life, and cursing her, though innocent, for entering my solitary existence and turning my purgatory upside down.

My hands snapped the wallboard off the nails that were holding it onto their wooden supports. In my fury I tore, pulled, and yanked the walls down until there was nothing left.

No holes. No walls. No reminder.

Nothing.

I stood, breathing hard, in the middle of the entryway. Sweat poured down my face, plaster dust clung to my wet skin and clothing. The air was thick with a white haze, the drywall bits covered the floor, beaten.

And still I could feel her presence.

I fell to my knees, the dust floating back into the air.

My arms itched from the powder coating my skin and I coughed, gagging on the chalky substance hovering in the air. Didn't matter. I deserved to suffer.

My body began shaking as I sat there in defeat. In the future I would mourn two losses of my love on that date: my wife and my Lila.

I wouldn't let what happened to her happen to Lila. I couldn't. Lila would live. Lila would meet someone worthy and start a family. Lila would be happy.

But not with me.

A sob erupted from my chest, startling me. The sting of tears in my eyes was disconcerting as my loss crushed me. I mourned them; one taken from me and the other I threw away.

Tears spilled down my cheeks, my body finally having had enough; enough fighting, enough feeling.

Enough.

————— ➤➤●❬●❭●◄◄ —————

The next morning my alarm went off, but I was already awake. My eyes were glued to the ceiling, staring blankly at the white expanse. In the time I was staring I noticed the nail pops, small cracks in the plasterboard, and the all-consuming ache in my chest.

I slept terribly; tossing and turning, fighting nightmares, and periods of insomnia.

As I laid there, I realized it was the first night in months that Lila wasn't next to me in the bed. Her delectable cherry blossom scent and warmth filling the room. It'd been months since I'd awoken without her soft body curled into mine, our limbs entangled.

Instead the bed was cold.

No good morning kisses.

No morning sex with my goddess.

No sweet smiles from my Honeybear.

No Lila.

My Lila.

An hour later, on autopilot, I was dressed and walking to my car. I noted hers was still in her parking spot a few down from mine. In the rearview mirror the dark circles around my blood-shot eyes made them stand out; evidence of my sleepless night.

I arrived at our office and breathed in her sweet scent that still lingered there. Sitting at my desk, I went straight to work and braced myself for her entrance. It was almost seven thirty; she would be there any moment.

Halfway through the Anderson contract and still no Lila. Odd, as it was a few minutes past eight. Then again, after what I'd done, I didn't expect her to come in early.

At eight forty-five she still wasn't there.

I checked my phone every few minutes to make sure I hadn't missed her call. My leg started bouncing in agitation. In my head I began to spin different scenarios of why she was late, some of them causing me to worry about what might have happened to her.

The Boob Squad left me alone, obviously noting my mood. Thank God, because there was no way I could deal with them that day.

By nine fifteen I was pulling at my hair, when Caroline stuck her head in to say good morning and stopped as she noticed the empty desk.

"Where's Lila?" she asked.

I kept my focus on my work, refusing to meet her eyes. "I don't know."

She closed the door behind her and her tone, when she spoke , contained enough force to draw my attention. "What do you mean you don't know?"

I shook my head, my brain trying to find the words so she could understand. "I couldn't keep hurting her, Caroline."

8

There was a knock on the door before Andrew entered. I watched his bright smile fade when he noticed the scene in front of him. "What did you do?"

I leaned forward, my elbows resting on the desk, my hands pulling at my neck. "I ended it. I hurt her, and then I ended it."

"You fucking moron!" Caroline screamed at me.

At the same time Andrew yelled, "I can't believe I fucking trusted her with you!"

Caroline's hand collided with my right cheek, and I welcomed the physical pain. "You...She's in love with you!" My head swung back to meet her fierce gaze, my eyes wide in disbelief. "Do you have any fucking clue what you've done?"

It felt like the floor was falling out from beneath my feet.

No, oh please no. Don't love me. Please don't let it be true. They'll kill you. They'll kill you like they did her.

"Give me your key and I swear to God if she...if she isn't all right I will kill you!"

I stared up at Caroline, believing her threat. "I don't have her key. I gave it back."

"And how did she take all of this?"

"I don't know. She passed out. I...I took her and placed her in her bed. I told her in a letter, though I'm sure she understood with my actions, and I switched out our keys before I left."

"You fucking coward!" Andrew said; every muscle was tense, and I wondered when he was going to hit me. I deserved it.

I flinched at his words, but agreed with him.

9

"We need to check on her and we need to do it *now*," Caroline said, pacing in front of me. "I'll call her cell, if she doesn't answer we are going over there and *you* will get us in."

I nodded in agreement, my chest tightening.

She was all right, she had to be. She was just upset. She'd be fine.

I tried to convince myself over and over. It wasn't enough. Opening up my desk drawer I pulled out my anti-anxiety pills and took one, then stuffed the bottle into my pocket.

Caroline wasn't able to get ahold of Lila, so we headed out, leaving word with Jack's assistant about the situation, leaving out the part about my relationship. The assistant hadn't heard from her either and confirmed she would alert Jack of the situation and our absence.

I let out a sigh that Jack wasn't available. I wasn't sure I could face him right then, or lie to him anyway. He knew me too well and could call my bullshit. One look and he would know. He would know that we were something more.

We all piled into my car and ten minutes later we were in the parking lot of our building. Her car was where I had last seen it, cool and unused, in her parking spot.

"Mike!" I called out as we rushed in and up to the desk. "Have you seen Lila Palmer today?"

"Lila? No, she hasn't come down yet," he replied, a bit bewildered by our entrance.

I began to shake, Andrew had begun pacing, and Caroline was biting at her fingernails. None of those were good signs.

10

"Can you ring up and see if she answers?"

"Sure thing, Mr. Thorne."

He let it ring nine times before hanging up and shaking his head.

"We need your help. Lila didn't show up to work and her car is still here. We're unable to reach her by phone and we're worried there's something very wrong. We need to get into her apartment and make sure she's okay; can you help us with that?"

"Well, we do have keys for emergencies," he said, his voice shaking and his jaw tense – making it obvious he was now infected with the same worry that plagued us.

"This is definitely an emergency." My voice cracked with the force of emotions.

Something was wrong. I could feel it in my bones. My inner beast that had been silent, brooding, was whimpering and pacing.

Please, please, be all right.

Mike unlocked a hidden safe behind the desk and pulled out a bundle of brass keys. Andrew wouldn't stop pushing on the elevator button, all in hopes it would get there sooner, and when it finally did, we all rushed in.

The soft elevator music could not dissolve the building tension as we climbed up to the twelfth floor. Mike was out first, and we followed behind to Lila's door, anxiously awaiting him to unlock it.

I was trembling, my stomach knotted. I felt like I was on edge and afraid of what we would find on the other side.

The door swung open and we burst through, all of us calling out for her.

11

"Lila!" I rushed toward the family room. In my peripheral I watched Andrew head right toward the kitchen and Caroline make straight for Lila's bedroom.

I stared after Caroline and a few seconds later her voice broke the fear. "In here!"

I stood frozen, afraid of what I was about to see. It shattered when I watched Andrew run out of the kitchen.

I rushed after him, my eyes frantic in their search for her as I entered the threshold.

The sight before me caused my knees to go weak, my legs threatening to give out, and my balance shifted my weight backwards into the door frame, my hands grasping it for support to keep me from falling.

No. No, no, no, no, no, no! No!

Please! Please, Lila, please!

No, no! Please be okay, please be okay!

My mind was frantic, begging for hope.

Lying on the floor near the foot of the bed was Lila; her hips were twisted, shoulders against the floor, arms splayed, head tilted to the side. She was naked, just as I had left her the night before.

Her pale skin showed the deep bruises of my body's assault on hers. I had been too hard, too rough, too much. I was out of control, and I knew it.

The world stopped – everything stopped – when I reached her eyes. Her beautiful gray-green eyes were open, the lids unable to close. They were glazed over, empty, flat, void.

Images of a night years before, another set of eyes, flooded my mind.

Empty.

Void.

Dead.

My stomach turned, and I propelled my body to the adjoining bathroom to heave into the toilet. I hadn't eaten so only bile and acid were expelled; my stomach retching to purge my mind.

My ears were ringing, and I couldn't hear anything that Caroline and Andrew had said from the moment I saw her lying on the ground.

Caroline's voice erupted, breaking through. "Mike, call 911! Oh, Lila!"

"Is she breathing? Please say she's breathing!" Andrew begged.

"She is! Lila? Can you hear me? Lila?"

I wiped my mouth and walked back into the bedroom where my Lila laid alive, but unresponsive.

"Goddamn son of a bitch!" Andrew roared before his fist collided with my jaw.

I stumbled back against the wall. His hand grabbed at my suit and brought me back up to face him.

"This is what you fucking said to her?" He held up the letter I'd left her. "I thought you understood her. I thought you cared for her. You fucking destroyed her!" He looked at me with absolute contempt and his tone was murderous. "You fucking stay away from her. You don't talk to her, you don't fucking look at her." For a moment I got a reprieve from his animosity as he turned to look at Lila's lifeless form. "Do you have any idea what you've done?"

"It's better this way," I whispered as Caroline covered her body.

"Like fucking hell it is! She was getting better, we could all see it. That was your doing. You were healing her. Now...she's barely functioning."

My stomach clenched again, my breath catching. "I warned her from the beginning. I begged her to go. I hurt her, Andrew."

"*You* did this to her. She trusted you. You know what happened to her and you just confirmed everything they ever told her. You knew how broken she was and you went and fucking crushed her. You were healing her, and now? She may not recover from this." He was seething, glaring down at me, his nostrils flared.

The room remained quiet after Andrew stopped yelling at me. We waited on pins and needles for the paramedics to come and take her away. I couldn't drive, and Andrew wanted nothing to do with me so he grabbed Lila's keys and took her car, while Caroline shoved me into my car and drove us. We arrived at the hospital not long after the ambulance.

Since I wasn't family they wouldn't tell me a thing no matter how many people I cursed, yelled and spat at. It was a nightmare, one from which I was afraid I might never wake up.

⇒•••●❲❳●•••⇐

Sometimes it was good when members of your family worked at a hospital, but sometimes it wasn't. The times when you screwed up and destroyed a beautiful woman – there they were without invitation.

My mother looked at me with such pity, while my father looked disappointed.

We'd been there about an hour when a familiar form was walking down the hall toward us.

"Darren?"

"Nathan?" Darren Morgenson, my therapist and friend, wrapped his arms around me in a hug. "What are you doing here?"

"I fucked up." The words slipped out, because that was all that was going through my head.

He pulled back and studied my face. "What are you talking about?"

"What are you doing here?" I asked, diverting talk away from me. I didn't think I had it in me to tell him I'd destroyed my own heart and an innocent one in the process.

"I got a call, one of my patients. Poor girl's had a breakdown, it seems." He shook his head. "I haven't seen her in months and now this. She's so fragile; I always wondered when she'd break."

My eyes widened and my stomach dropped. "Lila Palmer?"

He blinked at me. "Yes. How did you know?"

"He's the fucker who broke her," Andrew said from behind me, sticking his hand out for Darren.

"Hey, Andrew, how are you doing?" Darren asked, trying to hide the momentary look of frustration toward me, regarding my actions that caused all of the fuckery that was going on. His eyes shifted to Andrew.

I exhaled and my shoulders rounded forward, crumpling in on myself. Every moment away from Lila made my bones ache and my muscles tense up. Yet, there I stood—

rooted in place, helpless to do anything to change any of it. In addition, I was reeling from the information that Darren was both mine and Lila's therapist.

Andrew's lips were set in a thin line. "I'd be doing a lot better if Lila was at the office."

Darren nodded in understanding. "I take it you know what happened."

Andrew jerked his head in my direction. "Like I said, *he's* responsible. You'll need to ask him."

I tried to meet Darren's gaze, but I couldn't. I was drowning in my shame.

"What is he talking about?" Darren turned to me. "Look at me, Nate. What the fuck is he saying?"

"I had to." I managed to choke out the words.

"He left her this." Andrew handed Darren the note, and I cringed.

Darren gasped as he read it. My eyes flickered over to him, and I could tell he was furious.

He looked back at me, anger and pain in his expression. "You just undid six years of therapy in four sentences. Four fucking sentences!"

He stormed off down the hall to her room, leaving me to drown in my growing self-hatred.

It was not what I wanted.

We stayed for a few hours, but Lila never woke up.

Darren and her other doctors came out, looking for her family. None of us were, but Caroline lied and said she was her sister. Darren knew better, but he didn't correct her. They were sisters in spirit.

Self-induced psychological coma, they told Caroline. Lila had retreated into her own mind, unable to take the pain and harsh, new reality I'd created.

Days passed and Lila was still unresponsive, trapped in the recesses of her mind. For the second day in a row I found myself leaving the office at five and rushing over to the hospital.

Work was utter hell. I hated being away from her.

Nothing changed in the ten hours since I'd last been there. I walked into the room with quiet steps up to the bed. She looked so peaceful, like an angel. The constant beeping of the machines, along with the low rise and fall of her chest, put to rest the creeping fear that she was gone. Each breath and beat I clung to.

She was still there, alive, and she would return.

I hoped.

My hand reached out to move a stray strand of hair from her face, but I stopped myself. It was one thing to see her, to smell her, and to feel her presence, it was another thing entirely to touch her.

This was for the best, I reminded myself.

I turned and walked back out to the hall. Once there I leaned on the wall and stared at the room across the hall. A shiver ran down my spine and my body shuddered as memories flooded back to my mind.

I pushed them away and slid down the wall to sit on the floor. My mind turned over to the beeping of the machines that let me know my Lila was still with me. After a few minutes my heart began to beat in time with hers.

I sat there listening, thinking, feeling, until after midnight when a nurse came by and told me I couldn't stay any longer.

When I returned the next night her door was closed, and through the small glass window I could see Darren and a few other doctors looking at the monitors and talking.

Taking my position again I slid down the wall, coming to rest on the cold, hard floor. I closed my eyes, my head tilted back and I listened to the steady beep of the machines.

I heard the door to her room swish open then click closed. I didn't know if he saw me or not, but he knew I was there.

He sighed. "Why are you sitting out here? If you came this far, why don't you go in and see her? She knows you're here, after all."

My head snapped up. "She's awake?"

I watched Darren turn to look at me, a sad smile on his lips. "No, not yet."

"Then how do you know she knows?"

"Her heart rate's been steady all day. It picked up about fifteen minutes ago," he said, then quirked his brow. "How long have you been sitting out here?"

I stared up at him in wide-eyed shock. "About fifteen minutes."

"That's what I thought." Darren slid down to sit next to me. "What are you doing?"

"What do you mean?"

"Here. Why are you here? You broke her, yet you come by every day and sit outside her room."

I sighed. "I don't know. I just… I feel such a pull to be near her. I hate that I did this to her…but it's better this way."

"Better than what? You may be saving her from the possibility of being harmed by Marconi, but what do you call that in *there*? Three fucking days she's been unresponsive." He hitched his thumb toward her room. "In that room they're talking about moving her to a facility I don't want her to go to. She has no next of kin... Well, none that would come. She just has you and a small handful of friends. Friends who have lives. What do you have, Nathan?"

I sat there, staring at the room on the other side of the hallway.

He answered for me. "Nothing. You have nothing. You had her. A beautiful, broken woman who would have done anything for you. A woman who loves you, and you were selfish."

"*Selfish?*" My voice rose in indignation, my head snapping to look at him.

"Selfish. You did this for your protection more than hers. The thought of losing her the same way you lost your wife crushes you, doesn't it?"

"I… How do you know she loves me?"

"Way to deflect there, Nathan. Don't worry, I won't forget. And I know, because if she didn't love you, she wouldn't be in her current state. And if you didn't love her, you wouldn't be sitting out here in your expensive suit, on the floor, outside her door in a *hospital*."

I cringed at the word, just as he probably knew I would.

After spending months in a hospital after the accident, I hated them. The smell alone made me sick. Especially there, in that wing, sitting across the hall from the room that had once been my home.

There was a sudden shrieking plea that rang out from her room. Lila was screaming, begging. Darren jumped to his feet and threw the door open, rushing into the room.

I turned, my fists slammed on the wall while her screams echoed around the hall. My eyes were screwed tight, but the tears leaked through as I listened to my Lila cry out.

Her screams and pleas cut through me, tearing me. I wanted to run in and take her in my arms and never let her go. I wanted to chase away her fears and self-doubts. Declare my undying love, want, need, and support.

"No one wants me!" she wailed.

My heart splintered. "*I* want you," I whispered into the wall. I held my body tight and tense to keep me from running to her, to keep my heart from ruling.

I felt a warm hand on my fist, and I looked up through bleary tear-filled-eyes to find my mother staring down at me with a sad expression on her face.

"It doesn't have to be this way, Nathan."

"Yes, it does. She's safe this way…without me in her life."

I continued to listen to her pleas and sobs as Darren worked on calming her. It was my punishment. I had done that to her, I needed to hear it. Every cry and sob I created. I broke her.

My chest tightened, constricting my breathing.

20

It's better this way.
She's better off without me.

I repeated those words over and over in my head, trying to convince myself that I had done what was best for her in the long run. A mantra, as I remained in the hall, listening to everything that poured out of her. My heart broke more the longer I listened, but it was my punishment. I had to hear her pain, because she was what mattered most.

But if I walked through that door and saw her I might shatter. I'd much rather sit outside, listening to her scream, and let her be comforted by Darren. He knew what to do. He always did. I couldn't offer her any solace; I didn't have it in me anymore.

All my fucking fault. All of it.

⟫⟩⟩●⟨⟨⟪

They released Lila the next day, and I was left without any outlet to her. At least in the hospital I could be near her, but it was much better that she wasn't there any longer. However, I was not better.

The beast within me paced, and I grew restless. Sleep evaded me, and I was lucky to be getting three or four hours a night. It was never in one shot either; forty-five minutes here, thirty there.

When Monday rolled around, I was anxious yet elated. I would see her again, and maybe that would soothe me some. I was happy she was returning to work because that meant she was awake. Over the previous few days I found out just how much I'd grown used to always being around her, how much I was addicted to her.

21

I arrived at the office early, as the insomnia had me up before five, and anxiously awaited her arrival. I was a nervous wreck and had no clue what to do or how to act. I just knew I was miserable and I guessed that she was worse.

Worse was an understatement when she arrived a little while later. What walked through the door and into our office was not the Lila I knew. My heart ripped again. She looked...different. Almost as if she'd reverted back to that time in the parking lot. Her eyes were directed to the floor, hair down. She didn't look my way. She didn't acknowledge my presence.

It was difficult to look at her, knowing I'd done that to my Lila, but it had to be that way. Didn't it?

I could smell her and a calm spread through my every nerve. She was there, she was alive. That was what mattered.

Alive.

She continued to avoid looking at me while booting up her computer and sorting through the piles on her desk. Still no acknowledgement.

"Good morning, Lila," I said. I was going to say more, but refrained when she cringed. My chest burned, the knife twisting deeper.

It was better that way.

<hr>

The days passed just the same, silence prevailing between us. I hated it. Every moment was torture, and not just on me. Lila wasn't even trying to hide the pain, her façade blown away. Stuffing herself into work to avoid thinking, perhaps?

I knew that was what I was doing. Distracting myself with contract after contract.

On her fourth day back it was so busy I didn't even take a lunch break. I ran to the lobby, picked up a quick deli sandwich from one of the vendors that occupied the first floor, and ate at my desk. I almost picked up Lila's favorite, but I had a suspicion it was a bad idea.

She never left her desk, other than to get more coffee or some water. She drank her coffee black, so I knew she wasn't getting any calories there, and I hadn't seen her eat anything.

I glanced over at her and cringed. She'd lost weight over the last week. Not a lot, but noticeable. I knew I was to blame.

She's in love with you!

Caroline's words rang through, interrupting my thoughts.

There was only two hours left before she was to leave, Jack making sure she didn't overdo it, and I had a feeling she wasn't eating at home.

I knew I wasn't.

"Lila, go eat something," I said, my eyes never leaving the screen. I needed to stay detached to keep myself restrained. That was why I hadn't engaged in conversation with her since her return.

"No." Her fingers didn't even skip a beat on her typing.

My jaw twitched. "Go."

"I'm not hungry." Her voice was detached, but held the beginnings of annoyance.

I slammed my hands down on my desk.

23

Dammit!

In my peripheral she jumped, but kept her head down. I startled her. She did look my way as I stalked out and down to the break room. I surveyed the contents of the vending machine and found there wasn't much of anything healthy, but at that point she just needed something in her system.

Her favorite granola bar was there, so I entered my money into the slot. After retrieving it from the machine I returned to the confines of our office. I threw the bar onto her desk and it landed right in front of her.

"Eat it," I demanded.

"No."

"Eat the fucking granola bar before I shove it down your throat." It was taking all my control to keep from yelling at her; I was so angry that she wouldn't just take it.

Her hand wrapped around the package, and I smiled on the inside. My body sighed in relief that she was doing as I asked, but was quickly proven wrong when she threw it against the wall. It shattered inside the wrapper with a crack before falling to the floor.

"Oh, I've heard that threat before," she spat up at me. Anger was boiling in her eyes, venom lacing her tone.

My eyes grew wide as I remembered the last time I'd given her a similar threat. My chest ached, longing for the time when things were different between us. Times where my possessiveness was allowed to get the better of me, and my cock ruled.

Her anger was new, confusing, and I didn't know what to do. Something that scared me, but made me proud at the same time. I hated that she was going against me, but at the same time happy she was fighting back.

I'd taken to drinking at night, which was not good for anything that got in my path. The alcohol reduced my inhibitions, and the beast was let out. All my anger and pain unleashed upon my surroundings.

I wondered if I was like a drug addict going through withdrawal. I had all the symptoms, my physical dependence on Lila showing its ugly self.

My depression and anxiety spiked, and I craved her more than I ever had before. I *needed* her.

My condo was a mess, the drywall still laid on the floor in the entryway, various pieces of furniture were knocked over, and the closet in the master bedroom was ransacked. Clothes, shoes, belts were strewn all over the floor. Casualties of my search for something, anything, that was hers.

I emptied the hamper and found a shirt of mine she had thrown on one night and found it still smelled of her. I sighed, having enough of a fix to calm me somewhat.

I was a mess and it was my own fault. We could have been together, there were ways.

But there was no thinking on that day, only pain. It was for the best…for her.

We can give her what is best, what she deserves. We used to be that man, we can be him again.

Seeing her in the hospital, unresponsive, had been unbearable, but she was awake and she would get over me and move on. Get married and have a family.

25

Our *family. We could have been a family; we could have* made *a family with her.*

I shuddered at the thought, my eyes turning toward the small wooden chest lying exposed in the closet after my search. My mind moved back to another "made" family. My hand caressing the bump that lay between her hips, the ultrasound showing the life we had created.

Gone. All gone.

My wife.

My little boy.

"Happy birthday, Daddy!" she said with an excited smile while I opened the box she handed to me.

We were spending the weekend at her parents' place for a combination belated birthday-Father's Day party.

Within the box laid a black picture frame. Behind the glass an ultrasound picture with an arrow pointing between what appeared to be legs with the words "I'm a boy!" printed on it.

I smiled as I looked from my wife to the picture containing our child. Miscarriage after miscarriage, finally we were going to have our family. I leaned forward and captured her lips, conveying my love for her and for our child.

"I wish I hadn't missed that appointment."

"It was the first one you haven't been able to make. I think that's pretty good, especially with your schedule," she said, her hands running through my hair.

"But, I missed this." My fingers traced the form of our child.

"But what a great birthday slash Father's Day gift! Besides, you won't miss anymore."

I was pulled back by the frightening reality her statement held.

No, I didn't miss any more because there were no more to miss. She didn't know, none of us did, that just a few short hours later I would lose them both.

They said he wouldn't have survived outside the womb, even if he'd survived the crash and they'd gotten to him in time.

I saw the evidence photos; he didn't survive the crash.

I pulled the shirt back up to my face and inhaled, breathing in Lila's lingering scent. It was amazing how even that tiny bit that remained could calm me. What was I going to do when there was no more scent?

Her soft, warm body haunted me. I wanted to feel her in my arms. Just…feel her. Lila, *my* Lila.

My hand unconsciously rubbed at my chest to try and soothe the ache that lay beneath.

You can still fix this. Get her back! The beast spoke. *Lay claim to her, make her ours! Marry her!*

"No."

Why?

"And give Vincent Marconi someone else he can take from me?"

We can protect her!

I couldn't protect *them*; how was I supposed to protect Lila?

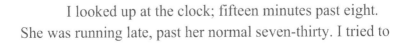

I looked up at the clock; fifteen minutes past eight. She was running late, past her normal seven-thirty. I tried to ignore the thought that sprung forth about the last time she was late, but it caught me nonetheless.

The phone on my desk rang and, in my daze, I answered it without looking at the caller ID.

"Nathan Thorne," I said in greeting. There was a whimpering on the line before Lila's voice broke through.

"N-Nathan, i-it's Lila."

There was something wrong, off in her voice, and I found myself on edge—my body leaned forward, bracing for the impact of her words.

"I-I'm n-not going to-to make it... Oh, God!" she cried out, and I heard the pain and fear. Mine was rising to meet hers. Her speech faltered, and I was unable to make out what she was saying. "Won't...be in..."

"Lila? Lila, are you okay?" My anxiety was skyrocketing faster than my heart rate. Her pain coming out in whimpers and gasps. She was having a difficult time breathing.

"So...ung...so much b-blood," she whispered more to herself than to me. "I d-don't know where...w-where it's com-coming from."

Her voice grew in pitch near the end. My stomach dropped and the blood fled from my face.

"Lila, what happened? Where are you?"

"C-crash. N-not far... St-t-star-b-bucks," she struggled to say.

I jumped up from my chair. Voices of the rescue crew were in the background, asking her questions, gaining vitals. What sounded like a chainsaw started, and I feared they had to cut her out of the wreckage.

Crumpled metal and mangled flesh flashed before my eyes and a vice formed around my chest then began to tighten.

"Lila! I'll be right there. Do you hear me? Lila!"

There was no response before the line went dead. I slammed the phone down on the receiver and ran out of our office. I rushed to the elevator bay and pushed the down button at a frantic pace in a fruitless effort for it to arrive faster. The doors sprung open, and I barely registered anyone was coming out as I pushed through and entered into the cab.

"Nathan!" Jack's voice rang out, drawing my attention. "Nathan, what's wrong?"

My eyes met his, and I knew he could see the fear and desperation. "Accident. Lila's been in an accident."

His eyes widened, but he remained silent as the doors slid closed. I didn't know how much I had just given away, but at that moment I didn't care; nothing else mattered. I needed to get to Lila, she was all I cared about.

I paced as the elevator descended to the plaza level and dashed out as soon as my body could fit through the gap in the doors.

Panicked, I ran. She was about half a mile away, and I could get there faster on foot.

I had to get to her, I had to tell her. I couldn't lose her.

Please...don't go!

The rain had let up to a sprinkle, but it didn't matter if it was down-pouring; I was too focused on reaching her.

I turned the corner, and it all came into view. Gawkers stood around, blocking me. Police cruisers were everywhere, fire trucks and ambulances, but I couldn't see her car.

I ran up to the line next to a cruiser when it came into view. The sight almost brought me to my knees, and it would have if the need to see her and make sure she was all right hadn't been so great.

It had been a direct hit to the driver's side. It was a crumpled mass of metal that once resembled her sedan. The door had been ripped off, and I could see blood on the upholstery.

That night began to flash again, overlaying on the scene in front of me. Another car, another crumpled bloody mess, with another woman I loved.

My heart rate increased and my chest tightened with each step forward, my body shaking.

"Hey, hey! You can't enter!" A cop called out to me, stepping in front of me.

"Please, I have to… Lila!" I yelled as I pushed past the officer. "Oh, God. Lila! Love, no! No!"

My vision started to darken and my heart was beating in my ears. It was sprinting. I knew the officer was trying to stop me, but I pressed forward, searching for her. Another officer came up and they tried to restrain me.

"Get your fucking hands off me. That's my girlfriend! Lila!"

An ambulance gurney came into view, and on it laid a woman. Her left hand was lying over the side, limp, stained with red.

"No!" I screamed, my knees buckling. Another image filled my mind, almost an exact parallel from the photo of my wife's hand to Lila's.

The officer attempted to slow my descent to the ground. My heart was beating at a furious pace, my chest caving in to the point that I was grasping, clawing, at whatever was keeping me from breathing. My vision was blurred and getting darker with each beat until I could see no more.

I had a vague feeling of people surrounding me, talking to me, and then I heard a familiar voice, breaking through everything.

"Help him! He's having a panic attack!" Caroline cried out.

I didn't even get to breathe a full breath before I felt a prick in my arm and everything turned black.

It was bright, sunny, and I had to shade my eyes from the light. Something stirred at my side and I looked down to find my Lila snuggled in. Her head tilted up; her intriguing gray-green eyes met mine briefly before snuggling back into my chest. My arm was around her shoulder, and I leaned my head down to breathe her in, kissing the top of her head. I let out a sigh and pulled her closer, reveling in her warmth.

I looked around and found we were outside, lying in the middle of a park, people all around us. People all around, yet there we lay, relaxed and content. I felt something move on my chest and looked down to find Lila's hand resting over my heart, a diamond glinting from her ring finger, a small band seated just beneath.

I couldn't pull her flush to me, so my gaze moved farther down and saw that her stomach was large and swollen. My hand reached out to rest on her belly. I felt a kick against my palm, and my heart swelled at the feeling of life beneath it. A life we had created.

She shifted and sat up. "Anna!" she called out. "Anna, come back away from the pond!"

I looked to where she called and my breath caught in my chest. A small girl, who couldn't be more than four, turned to look at us. Her light brown curls were bouncing as she ran toward us, hands waving in excitement. Her eyes lit up just before she threw her tiny body on top of me.

"Daddy! Daddy! There are fishies in the water!" The joy rolled off her tiny frame, her smile consuming her face.

Her unique gray-green eyes stared up at me, identical in color to Lila's. Her hair the same shade of brown as mine. Other elements of Lila could be found in the shape of her lips and the angle of her little nose.

My hand reached out to touch her face, but instead of meeting flesh, my hand fell right through her as she dissipated between my fingers.

The sky turned gray, dark clouds tumbling into view. My gaze turned back to Lila, she was still curled into me, but her body was limp and skinny, no swell in her stomach. I looked to her hand, it was now bare of the rings that had been there and blood covered her skin.

"Lila," I called to her, shaking her, but she didn't wake. "Lila!"

"Lila!" I cried out. My eyes snapped open, my breathing hard, as I looked at the ceiling. I could hear the beeping of various machines next to me.

I sat up and looked around, trying to orient myself, and recognized my family in the room. My mind fought back, trying to remember how I got there. Visions of Lila's crumpled car, her bloodied hand hanging from the stretcher came back at once. I swallowed back the bile that rose in my throat as the panic set in again.

I had to find her. I needed to make sure she was all right, that she was…alive. She had to be alive. Please, she had to be.

I pulled back the sheet and swung my legs over the edge. There was a tug on my hand, and I ripped the heart monitor from my finger. The machines began beeping wildly, alarms going off.

"Nathan, honey, it's okay. She's alive," I heard my mother say. I could tell by her tone it was a plea in hopes I would calm down, but it didn't work.

I could vaguely hear and see my parents in the room along with Darren, Trent, and Erin. They were talking in whispers, but I couldn't concentrate on that. I had to find her.

Please be okay. Please be alive. Please don't leave me!

"Lila!" I cried out for her, my panic rising.

"She's all right, Nathan," Darren said to me as he stepped to the side of the bed. I didn't believe him, I couldn't. I had to see for myself. I swatted at him, pushing him aside.

My feet landed on the cold floor, and I took a few steps forward before a sharp pain pulled at my wrist. I looked to find an IV line attached in one hand.

"Lila!" I called out again.

"Mr. Thorne, please, lay back down!" a woman in green scrubs directed upon entering my room. I ignored her, pushing past her and out into the hall, the IV tube in my hand as I dragged the stand behind me.

Darren followed behind me, arguing with the nurse; him telling her to let me go, her telling him I was disturbing patients.

I didn't give a fuck if I disturbed patients; *I needed* to find my Lila.

"Lila!" I called again. My chest was throbbing with each step, tears stinging my eyes. She had to be here, somewhere, she just had to be.

"Mr. Thorne! You need to return to your room!" The nurse screeched at me.

"He has to do this, Mary, just let him go," Darren said to the annoying nurse.

"Lila!"

The IV stand caught on something in the hall, and I pulled on the tube, dislodging it from the bag.

"Don't pull that out!" another nurse scolded as they all chased me down the hall.

"Lila!" I wailed. A sob was growing, about to release while tears began streaming down my face.

I looked into each room, one at a time, the irritating nurses following right behind, yelling at me, threatening me. Darren and my parents then started yelling at them.

"Lila!" I was begging for her to answer, but with each room I came to and didn't find her, my desperation grew.

My heart was hammering in my chest, the ache growing. My vision began to dim again, dread setting in.

I reached a room near the end of the hall, and leaned on the frame, bracing myself while my limited vision wildly searched for her.

And then I saw her. She was bandaged and beaten to hell, but she stared back at me with wide-eyed recognition.

My vision returned and my body relaxed while I took her in. Lila was alive. Thank God, she was alive.

Her eyes met mine, and relief flooded every part of me, tears stinging at my eyes. Joy that my nightmares hadn't come true.

I wasn't too late. I could fix this, fix *us*.

Made in the USA
San Bernardino, CA
06 April 2015